The Adventure of Craig and KJ

THESE ARE THE RULES

Written by

Trina Patterson

Illustrated by Avoltha.com

THANKS & DEDICATIONS

First and foremost, thank you God. My life is according to your will but thank you for continually opening doors and helping me through life and motherhood. To my mother, Vendetta Twine, you instilled a foundation in me that is unbreakable and that foundation will be passed down to your grandsons. My only regret is that you never had the opportunity to meet them. Bernice Pulliam (Nana), thank you for the love and exquisite taste, I know you're in heaven smiling down on us. Angie and Lisa Pulliam, thank you for picking up where my mother left off and never letting me go astray. I am the woman I am because of the both of you loved me unconditionally. Francine Brown, you were Lil Craig's first love and I can never repay you for the love and kindness you instilled in him, I hope you're in heaven guiding his steps. Chris G, thank you for always pushing me and encouraging and the boys, you are my best friend. Janise Beckwith, thank you for always supporting my ideas and dreams and all the long talks.

To Cheryl Bates, Mitzie Terry, Tiffany Mumphrey, Narita Singh, Jullita Matthews, Shaun Williams, Rarsha and Keith Evans, Mia Maddox, Shannon Kroger, Michael Woll, and John Klein, you guys are my TRIBE. You all at some point have kept me sane, helped me raise my children, made me laugh when I wanted to cry. You guys call me out when I'm wrong or fall short. I have taken lessons from all of you and am a better person because of each and everyone of you. To Raynita Anderson and Isaiah Hill, I love you both unconditionally.

To Kayla Williams, Maia Terry, Autum Catoe, Mauri and Maurche' White, Jada and James Brown, Shai Navarrez, Anari Hill, Bryce, Jace and Kayla and Kennedy Evans, you all come from greatness. Blaze all the trails life sets before you!

Love,

Trina

There's nothing greater than the bond between brothers, but when one brother is a little to eager to follow in his much older brothers footsteps- things go wonderfully awry. Follow Craig and KJ foible as they navigate the ups and downs of brotherhood and hold your breathe while KJ fumbles his way into big brother, Craig's shoes, one mishap at a time. These Are The Rules is a laugh out loud, feel good story about brothers, ten years apart in age, but undeniably connected and rooted in love, laughter and this thing called life.

* * * * * *

Thanks to my mom, KJ, Chris, Francine (Grandma), Brad, Mike Brown, Big James (Grandpa) Lil James, Jada, Chaka, Nelly (Godfather), Yomi Martin, James Twine Jr. (Papa), Kayla, Kyle, Sophia, Ms. Alex, Nanny, And Auntie Lisa. I love you guys. - Craig Brown

Thank you to Mommy's, Craigy, and Mickey Mouse - KJ

* * * * * *

To Craig and KJ:

You boys are my greatest accomplishment, my world. When I look at the both of you I understand how another human life can have the power to take over mine. I dreamt the both of you into life and while it isn't always easy, I wouldn't trade this journey with the both of you for anything. In life, I wish you both love, happiness, experience, family, wisdom, discernment and friendship. I pray you take the lessons that life will deal you with a humble and open mind and use them as stepping stones to better. Last but not least when you get the chance to sit life out or dance, I hope you dance, every single time you have the opportunity.

I love you both deeply!

Mommy ☺

I'm a teenager, so patience for me is hard,

but I love my little brother,

so, I have to teach him the rules.

KJ is little, so he doesn't always follow the rules,

but luckily, he has me, I'm Craig his big brother.

In the morning when you wake,

brush your teeth and wash your face

because these are the rules.

Always say please and thank you,

it's called being polite

and these are the rules.

Always eat your fruits and veggies

they help you grow up to be big and strong

because these are the rules.

Remember to wash your hands

after using the bathroom,

These are the rules.

You should share your toys when on a play date

Sharing is caring, and these are the rules.

When you make a mess

be sure to clean it up,

these are the rules.

Be happy and carefree

but more importantly be yourself,

exactly who you were born to be

because these are the rules.

Know that no matter what

you can always count on me

I will be there for you

because I'm your big brother

and these are the rules.

Don't forget before you go to sleep at night

to say your prayers and tell the universe your wishes,

oh, and be sure to give mom big goodnight kisses!

Because these are the rules

little brother.

www.ingramcontent.com/pod-product-compliance
Lightning Source LLC
Chambersburg PA
CBHW041013170626
46815CB00003B/284